WILBUR THE WALRUS

by **LAUREN LEDERLE**

illustrated by **ANTONELLA FANT**

To my amazing children.
Collin, Reese, Jackson, William, and Evan. Without you I
wouldn't have the imagination to finish this book.
And to my supportive husband, Jake. You were with me
20 years ago when Wilbur's character was born. You
gave me the push I needed to make this book a reality.

ISBN: 979-8-9883438-0-6

Illustrated and Designed by Antonella Fant

www.antonellafant.com

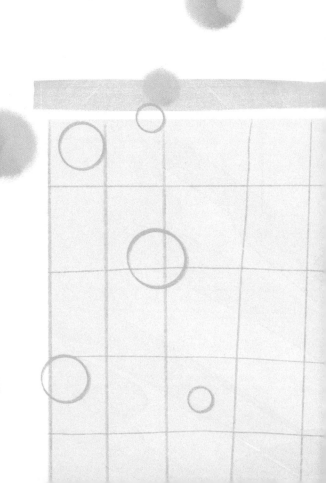

It started out as a typical Saturday morning.
I woke up before everyone else and went straight to the bathroom.

With a good stretch and a yawn I looked in the mirror and saw something in the reflection I didn't expect to see.

I rubbed my eyes to be sure that I was seeing correctly. I let out a yelp and he apologized.

"I'm sorry, I didn't mean to scare you. My name is Wilbur."

Then he put out his flipper for me to shake.

I was in such shock that I stammered

"H-h-hi, my n-n-name is Sam."

Before I could ask him what he was doing in my bathtub, he told me himself.

"I usually don't climb into peoples' windows you see, but I escaped from a nearby zoo and I didn't make it far before I wanted to go for a swim."

"Well, I planned to be out of your bathtub before someone woke up, I really did, but I realized I was stuck! Do you think you can help me?"

I stood there staring at him for what felt like an eternity. Was I dreaming? Not only was there a walrus stuck in my bathtub, but he could talk!

And why, oh why did he think he could swim in it?

I told him I would give it my best shot. I grabbed both of his flippers and pulled. He didn't move an inch! It hit me how ridiculous this was.

I am only 10 years old and definitely didn't have the strength to lift a...

2000 POUND WALRUS!

I pondered this odd situation for several minutes to try and come up with a solution. I knew I had to be very quiet and not wake my parents.

How could I get him out without making a lot of noise?

I decided to use bubble bath for my first attempt.
Surely soap would make it slippery enough for him to slide out.
I dumped the whole bottle all over him. Wilbur started to twist
his body.

There were bubbles everywhere! He wiggled and
wiggled, but couldn't get out.
It was almost too slippery!

My next attempt was a shovel.

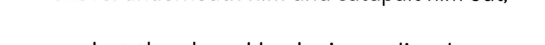

I thought with him being slippery with soap I could slide the shovel underneath him and catapult him out,

but the shovel broke immediately.

Here I was standing there with a broken shovel in hand, bubbles all over my bathroom, and no idea what to do next.

Then it occurred to me, a rope!

There was just one problem though. Where could I find one without waking my parents?

Not knowing what else to do, I decided to tie 5 of my sister's jump ropes together.

I threw the homemade rope in and tied it around Wilbur. This was no easy feat! I practically had to get in the tub to do it. I grabbed the other end of the rope and pulled with all my might!

I was huffing and puffing, sweating, and my arms were starting to hurt.

Yes, it must be working!

I turned around to see the progress I had made.

Nothing had happened! Nada!

All I saw was a disappointed walrus staring back at me.

Suddenly there was a loud sound. A cracking sound.

Wilbur and the tub were about to go through the floor!

I grabbed his flipper and tried to hold on, but down he went.

Looking through the new hole in my bathroom I could see that the downstairs was a mess, but Wilbur was finally free!

He gave me a thumbs up with his flipper as he brushed the bathroom floor off of him.

I raced downstairs to find Wilbur trying to clean up the mess. I told him he had to leave as soon as possible. I didn't want my parents to find him and send him back to the zoo.

Then I ran around my house to find things for him to wear.

I sent him on his way with my dad's trench coat, a hat, sunglasses, and a peanut butter and jelly sandwich. I figured he had to be hungry after all the ruckus.

He told me he was going to the bus station. Where to? I really have no idea, but that walrus had big plans.

As I waved goodbye I wondered if I would ever see my new friend again. But most importantly...

About the Author

This is Lauren Lederle's first book. Raised in Missouri, Lauren now lives in Texas with her husband, Jake, and her 5 wild and crazy kids. After receiving her Bachelor of Arts in Psychology, she chose to stay home with her children. Always on the go, most days you will find Lauren on adventures with her kids or serving as their personal taxi as she takes them to their abundance of activities.

Lauren has a vivid imagination. She has been creating characters from animals and telling funny stories about them since she was a little girl. It has been her dream come true to finally take the time to take one of these characters and turn it into a children's book.

About the Illustrator

Antonella Fant was born, and currently lives in Argentina. She is a visual designer, a children's book illustrator, and a concept artist, having studied Graphic Design and Illustration. Since a very young age, Antonella has been a self-driven person. As she grew up, her illustrations adopted a very similar personality as Antonella — childish, restless and curious. She took inspiration from TV cartoons and children's books that she used to read when she was a toddler. Antonella loves to create characters and stories to go along with them, and enjoys thinking as a child, drawing like them and for them.

Made in the USA
Middletown, DE
23 July 2023